Contents

The fox and the kitten

"It's a fine night," said Mrs Fox as she came up out of
her home. "A very fine night. What shall I catch for my
meal tonight? I'm so hungry."

She looked over at the farm.

"I'll find something to eat there," she thought.
"A good fat hen or a duck. Everyone will be asleep
and I'll take them by surprise."

But as she was running by the farmhouse, what should she see but a kitten. A thin little grey kitten.

Mrs Fox stood still.

The kitten stood still.

He looked at Mrs Fox.

"You won't make a very big meal for me," said Mrs Fox. "But you'll have to do. I'm so hungry."

"Oh, don't eat me!" said the kitten. "I'm too little for you. You're so big and strong, Mrs Fox."

"I know," said Mrs Fox. "But I'm very hungry."

"Then come with me," said the kitten. "I know where you can have the best meal you'll ever have in your life. Follow me."

So the two of them went through the sleeping farm until they came to the well. It was a big deep well with two buckets.

"Look down there, Mrs Fox," said the kitten, "and you'll see your meal."

Mrs Fox stood by the well and looked deep down into the water.

"Oh my!" she said.

She didn't know she was looking at a reflection, a reflection of the round full moon.

"What is it?" she asked the kitten.

"Cheese," said the kitten. "It's a big round yellow cheese. They always keep the cheese down the well on this farm."

Mrs Fox gave a gulp.

"How can I get down there?" she said. "I'm so hungry."

"Like this," said the kitten, and he jumped into the top bucket.

Down he went. Down, down, deep into the well. The other bucket came up. Mrs Fox waited. She looked down into the water again.

"Bring me up the cheese," she called. "I want my meal. Hurry up and bring me the cheese."

"I can't," shouted the kitten. His bucket was in the water, but he was clinging to the rope out of danger. "I can't. It's too heavy for me. You must come down and help me."

"Oh, really," said Mrs Fox. "What a silly little thing you are. I'll bring that cheese up in no time." And she jumped into the other bucket.

Down she went. Mrs Fox was so big and heavy that she went down, down, down and down.

The other bucket came up. The kitten jumped out.

He sat by the well. He washed his feet. He looked up at the moon, the big, yellow round full moon in the sky.

"It's a fine night," he said. "A beautiful fine night." And he went to sleep.

Nathan and the games on the moon

At school, Nathan was painting a picture. Miss Hill walked over to Nathan. She was his teacher. Nathan liked green paint, so a lot of his picture was green. There was also yellow and purple in his painting.

"That's a lovely bright painting, Nathan," said Miss Hill, "but I'm not sure what it is. Can you tell me?"

Nathan put down his paint brush and said,

"This is what the moon people look like. They have three legs and they are yellow, purple and green."

Miss Hill smiled. "I don't think people live on the moon, Nathan," she said.

Nathan went on with his painting.

"I know I'm right," he thought. "Miss Hill is just a grown-up. She doesn't understand."

That night, Nathan was in bed. He was reading a book before he went to sleep. Nathan looked at a picture on his wall. It was a picture of the moon. In his book, it said that people had walked on the moon!

"I hope I can do that one day," thought Nathan. "I'll make a rocket, a big red one. I'll fly up to the moon in it and play games with the moon people."

An owl flying outside Nathan's window looked in and saw Nathan asleep. He was dreaming. He was on the moon with his friends from his painting. They were very happy to see him.

"Let's play some games," Nathan said to them. First, Nathan ran in a race. To his surprise, his feet didn't stay on the ground. He was running in the air, and so were the moon people! Nathan won the race, even though the moon people had three legs!

Next, they all played leap frog. This was the best
game of leap frog Nathan had ever played. With every
jump he went higher up, up, up into the air.

"I'm flying! I'm flying!" he shouted. "Look at me!"

It was great fun. Then they played catch, and last of
all, hide and seek. The moon people hid behind the big
white rocks. Nathan found them because one of their
three feet always stuck out.

"I can see you!" he shouted, and he ran over to catch one of the moon people. Suddenly, he heard someone calling him.

"Get up, Nathan!"

It was Mum. He was back from the moon.

Mum came in and said, "Come on! You'll be late for school! What have you been doing?"

"I've been on the moon," said Nathan. "There are people there, just like in my painting."

"Oh, Nathan," said Mum. "You were only dreaming, you know."

Nathan thought, "Mum's just a grown-up. You can't expect her to understand."

At school, Nathan sat at a table with his friend Sam.

"I was on the moon last night," said Nathan.

"Didn't you see me there?" asked Sam, surprised. "I saw you! I was on my moonbike. The moon pirates were after me!"

Just then, Miss Hill came over. "What's all this noise?" she asked. "What are you two talking about?"

"There **are** people on the moon, Miss Hill," said Nathan. "Sam saw them, too."

"That's right," said Sam. "The moon pirates had a big black spaceship with a black and white flag. They were after me, but my moonbike was too fast for them."

Miss Hill just laughed, and Nathan could see that she didn't understand.

"Well, you're at school now, not on the moon," said Miss Hill, "and we've got lots of work to do. I want you all to start a nice big wall painting to put in the hall. I want you to do a picture about things you like to do."

"Can't we do a picture of the moon people and the pirates?" asked Nathan. "We like them."

"But you didn't really go to the moon," said Miss Hill. "I want you to paint something that you really do."

Nathan looked at Sam. They knew how real the moon people were. Nathan thought hard, and decided, "You have to help grown-ups a bit."

So he said, "Miss Hill, can we paint the moon people and the pirates if we call the painting *Our dreams*?"

Miss Hill didn't look at all sure, but at last she said, "Well, all right, then…"

As soon as she had gone, Nathan whispered to Sam.

"Miss Hill thinks we were dreaming, but I'll see you on the moon tonight. Us two can take on the pirates and we'll win!"

"Right," said Sam.

The mice who saved the moon

This is the story of how some of the earth's smallest animals help to save the moon.

Many years ago, before there were any people on the earth, the moon was always round and full. Her job was to light up the night sky with a soft light, just as the sun's job was to light up the day. The two of them were good friends and they shared the sky without any trouble at all.

But one night, as she shone brightly, a dark shadow fell across her face.

Shargath, the biggest, greediest dragon on earth had woken from his long sleep. He was hungry, and when he saw the moon through the clouds, he thought she might make a tasty meal. With a terrible roar, he flew at the moon and swallowed her in one go.

The night was suddenly much darker. The animals that were awake looked up in surprise.

"Where is the moon?" they asked. The owl, with his sharp eyes, saw the dragon flying away.

"There she is!" he said. "Shargath the dragon has swallowed the moon!"

The dragon flew off to his den in the clouds. He felt very full and he soon fell asleep. Down on the ground, things started to get very mixed up.

The sun saw that the moon had gone, and thought it was daytime. He started shining, but without the moon to help him, he didn't know when to stop, and he shone through day and night.

The animals that came out at night started to worry.

"What shall we do?" said the owls and the bats. "We sleep when the sun is up, and eat when the moon comes out."

"So do we," said the wolves, "and now we have nothing to howl at, either."

The badgers, moles and rabbits were also not happy. But the sun was saddest of all. Now that his friend the moon had gone, he had no time to rest.

So they all sat under the owl's tree, wondering what to do. At last the mice thought of something. In their tiny voices they told the others their idea.

"If we all work together, it might just work," said the wolves.

So they decided to try. They all set off to win back the moon from the dragon.

The bats and owls carried the smaller animals to the dragon's den. Once they were there, they made as much noise as they could. The rabbits thumped their feet, the owls screeched and the bats squealed. Down on the ground the wolves howled. As the terrible noise got louder and louder the dragon woke up.

"What's all this noise?" he roared.

"We want the moon!" shouted the animals. "And we're not going to let you sleep until you give her back!"

They started their noise again, even louder.

The dragon was angry. He tried to frighten them away, but with the big heavy moon inside him, he was too slow. He snapped and snarled, but he couldn't make them stop.

At the same time, the mice had crept round behind the dragon. With all the noise going on, he didn't even feel the mice chewing a hole in the end of his tail.

"Quick!" said the mice to the moon. "You can get out here."

And that is what the moon did.

She slowly squeezed herself through the hole that the mice had made. Bit by bit she crept out, first just a thin curve, then a half, until at last the whole of her was back in the night sky, shining down on all the animals. When they saw her, they cheered and left the dragon's den as fast as they could.

But when Shargath saw that the moon had escaped, he was furious. He flew up and swallowed her again. The animals were very angry, but then the mice said,

"Don't worry. He can't keep her this time. She knows how to escape now."

And that is how it has been ever since. Every month the moon slowly escapes, a little at a time. But as soon as Shargath sees her shining above him, he swallows her all over again.

That moon

That moon up there
in the winter sky
all spiked with stars
on a frosty night –
that silvery moon
sheds a brilliant light.

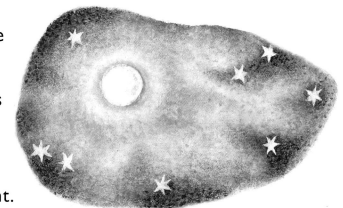

That moon up there
in the August dusk
when moths are drawn
to the window light –
that golden moon
is a marvellous sight.

That pale old moon
in the morning dawn
when the rising sun
spreads a rosy light
is a tired moon out
too late last night.

Ann Bonner

28

Reaching for the moon

"I wish I was taller," said Edward.

"You're all right just as you are, Edward," said Mum.

"I know I'm all right," said Edward. "I just wish I was taller, that's all."

Edward was small. All the rest of the children in his class at school were taller than him.

"If a magic fairy came down and gave me just one wish, I would wish I was taller," said Edward. "Taller than all the others in my class."

Mum laughed. "You're always reaching for the moon, Edward."

"What does reaching for the moon mean?" asked
Edward.

"It means to want something you can't have," said
Mum. Edward thought about that.

"I want to be an astronaut and fly to the moon,"
he said.

"There you go again!" laughed Mum. "Reaching for
the moon."

"Not reaching for the moon," said Edward. "Just
wishing I could go to the moon. And who says I can't be
an astronaut one day?"

On his way to school, Edward always went past Mr Bramley's shop, which was at the end of the road. Sometimes, if he had enough money, Edward would go in and buy some crisps or a comic. He would also look at the magazines.

"I'd like to be a racing driver," he said, looking at a picture of a racing car on the front of a magazine.

"Perhaps you will be, one day," said Mr Bramley.

That was what Edward liked about Mr Bramley.
He never said that Edward was reaching for the moon
when Edward said he would like to do something.
Mr Bramley always made Edward feel that anything was
possible. You only had to try and it might just happen.

"Do racing drivers have to be tall, do you think?"
asked Edward.

"I don't think so," said Mr Bramley. "There's not much
room in a racing car."

Edward smiled.

"I hadn't thought of that," he said.

"You could be a jockey," said Mr Bramley. "They have to be quite small."

"They do, don't they?" said Edward. He thought for a while, then said, "Yes, I should like to be a jockey and sit on a horse as it jumped over a big fence."

"And why not?" said Mr Bramley. "It might be fun."

"But I want to be an astronaut, too," said Edward. "Would it be all right to be both, do you think?"

Mr Bramley smiled.

"I expect so," he said. "I don't see why not."

That night Edward had trouble going to sleep. He tossed and turned, but still he couldn't sleep. He heard his mum and dad go to bed. He heard a dog barking somewhere. Much later, he heard a church clock strike midnight.

Edward got out of bed and pulled back his curtains. He looked up at the sky. There was the moon. Sometimes it didn't look very far away at all, as though you could put your hand out and touch it.

"I wish I could do that," thought Edward.

Something caught his eye. Not up in the sky with the stars but at the back of Mr Bramley's shop. What was it? A light moving? No, not a light, a fire! Mr Bramley's shop was on fire! And Mr Bramley lived over the shop!

"Mum! Dad!" shouted Edward, as he ran down to the telephone.

Edward didn't wait for his mum and dad. He just telephoned 999.

"Fire!" said Edward. "Send a fire engine!"

Mr Bramley was lucky. It was only a small fire and the fire fighters soon put it out.

"Well done!" one of the fire fighters said to Edward. "It could have turned into a big fire if you hadn't seen it."

"I was looking at the moon," Edward told him. "I like looking at the moon."

"It's a good thing that you do," said Mr Bramley.

Some days later, Edward went into Mr Bramley's shop on the way to school.

"I've got something for you," said Mr Bramley. He gave Edward a box. "It's to say thank you. After all, you did save both my shop and me."

"I didn't expect anything," said Edward. "What is it?"

"Look inside and see," said Mr Bramley.

So Edward opened the box and looked. He took out
what was inside.

"A telescope!" he said.

"It's a special sort of telescope," Mr Bramley said.
"It's very strong so that you can look at the stars – and
the moon, of course."

"Wait until Mum sees it," said Edward, smiling.
"She says I'm always reaching for the moon. Well, if I
look through this, I won't have to reach so far!"

The rabbit in the moon

Once upon a time, so the old Japanese story goes, a man lived all alone on the moon. Night after night he looked down at the Earth and wished that he could find someone to keep him company.

"It would have to be someone very kind," thought the man in the moon. "It would have to be the kindest creature of all to come and keep me company."

One night as he was looking down at the Earth,
a forest caught his eye. It was tall and green and full of
moonlight and there he could see three animals living
together – a fox, a rabbit and a monkey.

"How happy they look, and how kind," thought the
man in the moon. "Perhaps one of those is the kindest
creature of all."

Well, he looked and he looked but he couldn't tell by looking, so he decided he would have to go and find out for himself.

He turned himself into an old beggar man and slid down a moonbeam to where the animals were. The fox, the rabbit and the monkey all gathered round.

"Oh dear, oh dear," said the old beggar man. "I'm so very hungry. Please could you help me to find something to eat?"

"Of course we will," said the animals, and they all ran off to try and find food.

The monkey climbed to the top of the trees and soon she was back with her long arms full of the fruit she had picked. She put it down at the old beggar man's feet.

"This is for you," she said. And the man in the moon was very pleased.

The fox ran to the river and caught a big fish.
He carried the fish carefully back in his mouth and put it
down at the old beggar man's feet.

"This is for you," he said. And the man in the moon
was very pleased.

And what about the rabbit? Well, poor rabbit was hopping about the forest floor looking for food but all she could find were sticks and grass, food for a rabbit, but not for a man.

"Oh dear! What shall I do?" she cried. "The poor beggar man is so hungry."

Then she had an idea. She gathered up all the sticks and bits of wood she could find and carried them back to the monkey and the fox.

"Dear monkey and fox," she said, "would you help me to light a fire?"

"Of course," said the monkey and the fox.

Soon there was a good cooking fire going. Then rabbit turned to the old beggar.

"I couldn't find any food for you and I can't bear to think of you going hungry. So I'm going to jump into the fire and cook myself for you to eat."

And she turned back to the fire, all ready to jump.

Well, the old man in the moon couldn't let that happen. Quick as moonlight he turned from a beggar back into himself.

"Stop!" he cried. "Please don't harm yourself! Your kindness is all the food I need. I really think that you must be the kindest creature of all. Will you come and keep me company on the moon?"

"Yes," said the rabbit, who really was very kind. "Of course I will."

So the man in the moon picked up the rabbit in his
arms and flew back up the moonbeam to his home. And
there the two have lived happily ever since.

If you look up at the moon on a clear night, you might
even see the rabbit in the moon for yourself.